Reema Unveiled

Marshatta Rose

Published by Marshatta Rose, 2024.

REEMA UNVEILED

First edition. December 28, 2024.

Copyright © 2024 Marshatta Rose.

ISBN: 979-8230145943

Written by Marshatta Rose.

Table of Contents

To those who have felt trapped in love that hurt more than it healed, this is for your bravery in choosing yourself.

To the survivors who carry scars, visible and unseen, may you find strength in your story and hope in your future.

And to the people who stood by me when I didn't have the words, thank you for teaching me what love truly means.

Prologue

I first met him at a café. He approached me with a confident smile, his dark eyes alive with charm, and asked, "Mind if I join you?" Startled, I looked up but quickly nodded. "Sure, go ahead."

We talked for hours, the conversation flowing effortlessly. Louvel was magnetic—attentive, funny, and interested in everything I had to say. He noticed the way I tapped my thumb when I was nervous. Pointed it out, smiled, said it was endearing. No one had ever caught that before.

As our relationship grew, Louvel opened the door to a life I'd never imagined. Romantic dinners by candlelight, spontaneous road trips, and whispered secrets late into the night. His apartment became our sanctuary, a cocoon of stolen moments where it felt like the world couldn't touch us. For the first time, I felt understood.

But then, subtle shifts began to creep in. Louvel's protectiveness, once endearing, became suffocating. His concerned questions turned pointed. "Who were you with?" he'd demand, his tone sharp. "Why didn't you answer my call?"

I brushed it off, convincing myself it was love. *He just cares about me,* I told myself. *He's only worried.* But as the months turned into years, the cracks in our relationship widened. His temper, once rare, flared more often. His words—once sweet and reassuring—grew cruel, laced with accusations.

The man who made me feel safe now filled me with dread. The laughter and love that had once defined us were replaced by apologies that felt more like weapons. Every argument ended with promises that things would change, but the cycle always repeated, leaving me feeling small, silenced, and trapped.

I clung to the memories of how it all began—the way his smile lit up the room, the dreams we'd painted for our future. I told myself the man from the café was still there, somewhere. I just had to be patient. I just had to try harder.

But as I sit now on the cold hardwood floor, knees pulled to my chest, blood trickling from my nose, I know better. Tears streak my face, and my heart pounds in my chest as I listen to Louvel's heavy footsteps echo in the hallway.

The man who once made me feel alive has become a shadow that suffocates me. The love that lifted me up has turned into chains, and the home we built together feels like a prison.

I don't know how it came to this—how I let it come to this. But I do know one thing: I have to get out. Not just out of this apartment, but out of the darkness he's pulled me into.

1.
Fighting Tears

My breath is fast and sharp. I can't stop looking around, desperate for a way out. I need to leave, I need to get out, but I don't know how. Louvel's voice floats in from the next room, soft but threatening, "Reema, come here." Time's ticking. He'll be back any second. The front door feels like it's miles away. The bedroom's too close, escape feels impossible. Louvel's apartment—it's a trap. The walls are closing in, suffocating me.

His footsteps are louder now, closer. He stood in front of me and crouched down.

"Did you hear me? I said, come here." His voice is harsher.

He reaches for my arm, and I flinch away, wiping the blood that trickled down my nose to my neck.

"Don't touch me," I mutter, my voice shaking. I scramble to my feet, grabbing my phone, and wallet from the floor. No time for my stuff in the bedroom. I need to go now.

"Re, you know I'm sorry. Please come to the room," Louvel says, stepping closer. "I didn't mean it; You just— you just kept getting in my face" His words filled with desperation.

This is too familiar—him blaming me for his mistakes, twisting everything around. It was always the same. "Who was he?" he'd yell. "No one!" I'd say. Then the hitting, the shouting, the tears. But this time, something's different. I can't take the pain, not anymore.

Silence falls between us. Tears blur my vision, thoughts stabbing at my mind. How did I end up here? Memories of happier times mix with the harsh reality. Doubt and despair cloud my mind. *Can I really leave?* The question lingers.

I force myself to look up at Louvel, but my eyes only reach his chest. Fear anchors my gaze, but anger starts to boil inside me. *No.* I think to myself. My face twists in disgust.

"You didn't mean it," I say, holding up my blood stained hands. "You broke my fucking nose!"

I grip my keys tighter and step back toward the "I can't do this anymore."

I pause, knowing what could happen if I say the next part. I take a breath. Brace myself.

"I'm leaving."

Louvel's face darkens. His eyes narrow. Lips curl. He steps closer, and I know I have to move—now. His silence is deafening. I almost prefer the shouting.

I make it to the door. Almost.

Then he grabs me.

Not hard. Not fast. Just... certain. Like he's practiced it.

His arms coil around my waist, dragging me back before I can think, before I can scream anything that makes sense.

I hear myself yell, but it sounds distant. Hollow.

"No, not again."

The words barely feel like mine.

I twist, kick, claw for the floor. Anything. I hit the ground. Then the couch. Then the weight of him is on me again.

I stop hearing. Everything turns to static.

"Re, stop."

"You're not leaving."

"Not after everything."

His voice blurs in my ear, tangled with the buzz behind my eyes. I don't remember when I stopped fighting. Maybe I didn't. Maybe I froze. My brain folds in on itself, pulling away like it always does. Like it's trying to protect me.

I focus on the ceiling. That dull beige. The crack above the hallway light. I stare at it until my head hurts.

You've been here before.

He's not sorry.

You know that.

He's talking again. Softer now. His voice like a lullaby soaked in guilt.

"I love you."

"Look what you made me do."

"I didn't mean it."

I don't answer. I don't move.

Eventually, he disappears. The bathroom light flicks on. The sink runs.

I stay curled on the couch. Every limb heavy.

He comes back with a towel. He dabs at my skin like he's erasing something. His hands too gentle. His apology too quiet.

Then he wraps around me again. Arms like comforters. Like chains.

An hour passes.

I take my chance.

I slip out from under him, slow and careful. Each step a weight. I freeze when he shifts, hold my breath until he settles.

Then I move. Fast. Quiet.

Hand on the knob.

Out the door.

In the hallway, I remember my phone is still by the kitchen. *There's no chance going back now*, I think, as I run down the hallway, down the stairs, and into the street.

The early morning darkness is dotted with flickering streetlights. I wander aimlessly, my footsteps echoing in the empty city. The cool air bites at my skin. I shiver and rub my hands together for warmth.

I turned left, then right, then back again—my feet dragging like they couldn't decide either. Every street sign looked unfamiliar, every sidewalk too long. I walked just to walk.

Eventually, I sit on a bench. The silence settles around me, thick but not hostile. And in that quiet, a strange clarity washes over me:

I don't want to go back.

I can't go back.

I rise. Start walking again. I find my way to a hotel. I check my pockets—wallet. Relief hits like a wave.

This could be worse, I think, pushing through the glass doors.

Inside, the lobby is warm and soft and golden. Light spills from elegant chandeliers.

There's the scent of fresh flowers, faint coffee, polished floors. A piano plays gently from somewhere overhead.

I take a moment.

Steady myself. Try to blend in.

I approach the front desk. The receptionist—a young woman—is busy typing something. I clear my throat to get her attention.

"Hi." I say, trying to steady my shaky voice.

"Hello—" she begins, as she looks up at me, startled. She hesitates before continuing, "How may I help you?"

"Can I get 1 room, for Reema Barrett?" I reply, puzzled by her startled expression.

"Yes. Um—" she hesitantly gives me a tissue.

I immediately touch my nose, looking at the blood starting to cover my hands again. My stare fixates on it for a moment, as the memories of what happened starts to cloud my mind.

The receptionist shifts in her seat, taking my attention once more. I wipe my nose quickly, trying to get myself cleaned up. I forgot how beat up I looked. "Right. Yes. I got into a— a bit of a situation," I stammer, mostly to myself. I remember Louvel saying my nose didn't seem broken, but if that was the case why is it still bleeding?

She looks at me with concern, gets up, and grabs the tissue box. As she walks over, I notice her figure. She has a small frame but is generously curvy. Her hips sway as she walks towards me.

"Do you need me to call the police?" she asks, trying to help me clean up the blood.

No, it's fine. I just need a room," I say, taking the tissues.

She returns to the desk, anxiously typing. "Let me check what we have available."

Her hair falls over her face as she types. She tucks it behind her ear, annoyed by it. I find it cute. Her short brown hair has light highlights that falls just above her shoulders, and her glistening light brown eyes, in the light, looks like amber. Bold red lips standing out against her tan complexion.

I don't realize I'm staring until she looks up at me. Flushing with embarrassment, I look down to hide my face.

"I can get you into room 315. I'll call room service now to bring you a first aid kit."

"Thank you, but—" I pause, pulling out my card. "How much will it be?"

She shakes her head., "Don't worry about it," she says as she hands me the keys.

"Thank you."

As I start to walk away, I stop and ask, "Before I head to my room, could I get your name?"

She looks surprised but answers, "Oh, it's Lila– Lila Cielo."

"Well, that's a beautiful name. Thank you, Lila," I say, waving goodbye before walking away. I see her tuck her hair behind her ear again in the reflection of a mirror that sits in front of the desk, a soft smile on her face as she calls room service. *A beautiful name for a beautiful girl*, I think, until guilt hits me. What am I doing?

I walk toward the elevator, guilt pushing away thoughts of her smile. Once I reach the third floor, my body aches again, reminding me why I came to this hotel. I get to my room and immediately head to the shower. I sit in there for hours, scrubbing my skin in the hot water until it feels raw. The haunting memories replaying in my mind again and again. Tears roll down my face. The realization of my decision hangs heavy in me, but what he did is heavier.

I stay in the bathroom, trying to gather myself and figure out who to call and where to stay while I find a new place. I had moved in with Louvel a year into our relationship, leaving everything behind to be with him. Now, I have to start over.

The sound of room service knocking at the door pulls me back to reality, I leave the bathroom and open the door. They hand me a few supplies and reassuringly tell me that I could call whoever I needed on the guest room phone, pointing towards the bedside table. I thank them, then close the door and lay on the bed, staring at the phone.

"Who can I call? Asmin? Maybe, but she's probably asleep right now and who knows what she will say."

Then a thought hits me, *Maybe I could call dad.* I had tried to keep my distance from him while I was with Louvel, but I know he's the only person who will pick up.

I pick up the phone, trying to remember his number. "332-842... no. 332-412... ugh." I slam the phone down, and take a breath.

I try another number that comes to mind, hoping, praying it's his. Anxiously, I wait until someone picks up.

When the phone picks up, a deep, familiar voice answers. It's him. Even after all this time, I can't seem to forget his voice.

"Hello?" I hear from the other end of the line.

With my voice trembling I respond, "Dad? It's me."

"Mimi? It's been so long, where have you been? Where are you?" His voice filled with happiness but concern.

"I—I left him. I left Louvel. I don't know what to do now, I don't have anywhere to go."

He sighs before saying, "Love, let me come and get you. Where are you now?"

"I'm at a Easton-ridge Hotel."

"Alright. I'll be there soon just wait for me, okay?"

"No!" I yell before pausing. "Sorry, I just— don't come right now. Can you just pick me up on Friday."

"Okay..." He replies, sounding unsure.

"Okay. I love you, Dad. See you then."

With a hint of uncertainty, he replies, "Alright. I love you too. I'll see you on Friday."

I hang up the phone, setting it back down. I lay down on the bed. Holding myself together in a ball, the tears start again. I hadn't talk to my dad in so long, and he still is willing to drop everything to come and help me.

After a moment, I remember my phone is still at Louvel's house. I'll have to get a new one, I think to myself as I drift off to sleep.

2.
Going Home

The next morning, I wake up, barely recognizing my surroundings. *Right, I left*, I remind myself as I get ready. It's Thursday, so I have until tomorrow morning to pull myself together before my dad arrives to take me home. A sense of dread fills me as I think about seeing my mother again. I've managed to avoid her for the past three years, but now, there's no getting around it.

I throw on the hoodie I wore the night before with a pair of jeans, and head down to the lobby, where I pass Lila on my way out. She's busy typing away at the computer, so I just give her a soft smile and a wave, trying not to interrupt. She looks up with those pretty eyes, smiling and waving back. Butterflies fill my stomach. I really need to stop, I think, amused, though I'm not sure I'm doing this consciously. Maybe I just crave the warmth in her eyes, a welcome kindness I haven't felt in a long time.

Once I leave the hotel, I pull out the to-do list I made this morning. Buying a new phone is at the top. I can't do much without one, and I'm definitely not going back to Louvel's house—not without my dad, at least.

I take a taxi to the nearest mall, wandering around until I find a phone store. I grab the latest model they have; I've been wanting an upgrade, so I guess this works. As I stand at the counter, waiting for the employee to finish setting it up, I feel an odd mix of relief and fear. This phone feels like a fresh start—a small, practical step toward reclaiming my life. Yet, I can't shake the thought of Louvel noticing I'm off the radar.

Phone in hand, I wander the mall, the noise of people milling about around me both grounding and overwhelming. I'm alone, yet I feel eyes on me everywhere, suspicious glances that remind me of Louvel's piercing stare. My fingers clench around my phone as I breathe in, trying to ground myself, remind myself that he isn't here, that he can't reach me.

A few more stops—a change of clothes, toiletries, little things I left behind in my rush to escape. I pay with a mix of relief and shame. Each purchase feels like freedom, yet I can't help but wonder if I should even be here, moving around in broad daylight as though nothing happened.

As I step outside, the sunlight hits my face, bright and unyielding. It's the kind of light that forces you to confront the truth—no shadows to hide behind. Tomorrow, when I see my dad, I'll have to confront everything, and I know he'll ask questions I'm not ready to answer. He'll see the bruises, and as much as I want to tell him everything, I fear how he'll look at me afterward, what he'll think of the person I've become.

I take a deep breath, feeling a pang of nostalgia for a life that feels like a distant memory. I picture my dad's expression when he sees me—a mixture of relief, worry, and, no doubt, disappointment. It's the same look he used to give me whenever I came home late or failed a test, a look that cut deeper than any words ever could.

The street feels too bright, too real. I pull my hood up, tucking my face away as I walk back to the hotel, feeling the weight of tomorrow press down on me.

By the time I make it back to the hotel, it's already late afternoon. I sit on the edge of the bed, staring at my new phone, debating whether to call my dad and check in. I wonder if he's told my mother yet. Part of me hopes he hasn't, that I can somehow show up tomorrow without any problems. But I know my mother—she'll have prepared her reactions and her criticisms, all polished and ready.

A memory flickers through my mind: her disapproving glare the last time we spoke, the way she dismissed my relationship with Louvel as a "distraction" from what I should be doing with my life. I can almost feel the sting of her words, how they lingered long after I left home.

She reacted as if I'd dropped out of school, like I was throwing my life away. But I finished school, earned my degree, and got a job. Will she be happy with the degree I chose? No. But it's something I worked hard for. She wanted me to be a doctor; I wanted to be a photographer, so I became one. She took it as a personal insult, another act of defiance. But to me, it was finally doing something I loved. Photography was always a dream, and I made it real.

The more I think about it, the more I start to regret calling my father. Maybe going home wasn't the best idea, but it's my only way out—the only chance at being "free," at least from Louvel. I know I won't be free once I'm home, but at least it's a step in the right direction.

After pondering my decision for a while, I decide to stand firm on it. This is the only way I can live the life I want to live. By the time I settle on my choice, it's early evening, my stomach is growling, and a headache is starting to throb behind my eyes. I grab my phone to order some food and then head to the shower.

As I undress, the bruises catch my attention—reminders of my condition and just how bad it really is. I step into a cold shower, hoping it'll ease the bruising. Later, I take the ice from the bucket that came with the champagne I ordered, pressing it gently against my skin. I run the ice along my face, down my arms, and across my thighs. It stings, but the swelling begins to fade.

Afterward, I sit on the bed, watching TV while I eat. It's comforting to have time to myself—no one pushing me to do anything, no arguments over petty things, just silence. I'm not on edge, waiting for the next flare of anger or accusation. Just quiet, a moment where I can simply breathe. I realize how foreign this kind of peace feels, like I'm discovering it for the first time.

I let the sounds of the TV fill the room, something lighthearted to drown out the lingering memories of his voice. As I finish my meal, a warm drowsiness settles over me, and I let myself sink into the bed, savoring the calm. For the first time in what feels like forever, I can drift into sleep without fear.

This is what I want for the rest of my life, I think, letting my eyes close. To just be at peace. A life where I answer only to myself, where I can wake up each day knowing that I am safe and free to be who I am. The thought brings a soft, almost involuntary smile to my lips. For the first time, it feels like something I can reach—something real and within my grasp.

The next morning, I jolt awake from the ringing of my phone. I squint at the screen, still half asleep, as I hear my dad's voice mumbling on the other end. I catch only the last part of what he's saying, "...I'm outside."

Panic starts to set in, I jump up so fast I nearly fall face flat on the ground. My heart races, as I rush to the bathroom. "Okay, I'll be down in a minute," I say, trying to keep the tremor out of my voice as I frantically hang up the phone and run a brush through my tangled hair.

I catch my reflection in the mirror—dark shadows under my eyes, bruises, and the blood trickling down my nose again. I look a mess. I jump in the shower, scrubbing away at my skin. I wash my hair and throw it in some rollers I had bought the day before.

My hands tremble as I try to do the routine that's been ingrained in my head. Ice to calm the redness, followed by moisturizer to bring a soft glow to my skin. I layer on color corrector to mask the dark circles and bruises, then blend concealer to match my skin tone. Finally, I add lashes and lipstick, pulling it all together.

Once my makeup is finished, I move on to my hair, quickly drying the curls. They're not as polished as usual, but a messy bun will do for now. A spritz of perfume and a layer of body cream give me an air of composure. I slip into the new black dress I bought, pairing it with a brown fur coat and my gold earrings, necklace, and bracelet. I throw on my heels and for a moment, I feel almost normal when I look in the mirror.

I pack up the last of my things. pausing at the door, taking one last look at the hotel room. I clutch my bags tightly, the weight of them grounding me as I make my way down to the lobby.

As I step off the elevator, I see him almost immediately. He's sitting near the door, staring out the window, but the moment he hears the ding of the elevator, his head turns, and his eyes meet mine. His face lights up, full of excitement and relief. My heart pounds against my ribs, and I force a shaky breath.

"My little girl, it's been so long," he says, his voice filled with warmth as he stands up and makes his way over, arms stretched out. "Look at you—you've grown so much."

I can feel his arms wrap around me the strength and familiarity in his hug, and it nearly undoes me. My throat tightens, and tears start to swell up in my eyes, struggling to find my voice. "Hi, Dad," I manage, but the words feel weak, barely making it past the lump lodged in my throat.

The familiar scent of his cologne fills the air— a mix of cedar and something faintly sweet. It's comforting, yet it brings an ache. My hands grip my bags a little tighter as I pull back, hoping he won't see the worry etched into my face or the pain I start to feel from him gripping the bruise on my arm to tightly.

Through the ache, I can't help but remember my nose—it might still be broken. *What if it starts bleeding again?* The question floods my mind. I glance at myself, trying to seem composed, almost perfect, as if nothing is out of place. But one wrong move, and he'll know something is off.

I take a step back, slipping slightly out of his grip. His puzzled expression sharpens.

"Is something wrong, Mimi?" he asks, reaching toward me.

I quickly step back again, forcing a smile. "Yes! I'm fine. These bags are just a bit heavy."

"Oh! Let me take them, then!" he says eagerly, grabbing the bags from my hands before I can protest.

We walk to his car—an old relic from my teenage years, unchanged since I was fifteen. A wave of memories rushes over me as I take in the familiar black exterior, the beige leather interior, the lingering scent of his cologne mixed with faint cigar smoke.

Sliding into the passenger seat, I watch as he loads the bags into the trunk. Once he settles behind the wheel, we pull onto the road. It'll take about an hour to get back to the house. An hour of silence, I hope. I twiddle my fingers, willing the time to pass quietly.

After about five minutes, he breaks the silence, his voice careful but curious. "So, how's life been since school? How's your career- How's photography been treating you?" It feels like he's trying to bridge the years we've lost, so I give him bland, safe answers.

"Life's been good," I say, the words slipping out before I can stop them. I regret it instantly. He knows better. If everything were fine, I wouldn't have called him after all these years. Scrambling to recover, I add, "My career's going well. I've been focusing more on street photography than portraits. Actually, one of my pieces was published in a local magazine recently!"

The words tumble out, faster and faster, transforming my simple answer into a ramble. I start talking about my work, getting lost in the memory of seeing my photo in print for the first time, the excitement and pride it brought me. For a brief moment, his smile—genuine and proud—pulls me back to the past. It feels like old times, when car rides were filled with dreams I'd share freely, long before Louvel, before Mom and I started fighting. Back when life between us was peaceful—before it all fell apart.

"I'm happy things have been going well for you, Mimi," he says, but then pauses, his smile fading slightly. It's as though he's searching for the right words, trying to tread carefully. I know what's coming. "You called me so suddenly, and I'm glad you did. But... you didn't sound okay. Is something going on? Why did you leave Louvel?"

My breath catches, and I feel the weight of his question settle over me. How can I tell him? How do I explain the years of pain, the bruises, the isolation? That I left Louvel because he's been hurting me all this time? Tears prick my eyes, and no matter how hard I try to stop them, they spill over, streaming down my face. The mask I've carefully kept in place begins to slip.

I wipe at my tears with trembling hands, but it's too late. He glances at the rearview mirror and spots me, his voice instantly filled with urgency. "Mimi, what happened, my love? What's going on?"

"A lot, Dad," I whisper, my voice breaking as I swipe at my cheeks, smearing the makeup I had so carefully applied.

I reach into my purse, pulling out a compact mirror. Desperately, I fix my makeup, dabbing at the smudges and cracks, masking the truth again before he can see what lies beneath.

The car falls into silence, except for the hum of the engine. My hands tremble as I tuck the mirror back into my purse. My dad doesn't press me right away; he knows me well enough to recognize when I need time to find the words. But I can feel his eyes flickering toward me in the rearview mirror, his concern palpable, his lips pressed into a thin line.

We pass a gas station, and he glances at the tank. "Let's stop for a minute," he says, gentle, pulling into the lot.

This is his way of reassuring me, giving me the space he knows I need. He used to do this often when I was younger—creating small errands, quiet pauses, just to give me a chance to clear my head. I step out of the car, the cold air biting at my skin, sharp and unforgiving. Pulling my coat tighter around me, I'm thankful for the distraction, the excuse to look away as he fills the tank.

The light above the pump flickers, casting shadows across the pavement. It's only now that I realize the it's still dark outside. I glance down at my watch, its glow faint but steady: 5:36 a.m.

I feel him watching me, though he doesn't say anything. I hear the pump click, then he steps towards me. "Do you want anything? Water? Something to eat?" he asks gently.

I shake my head but pause, my voice barely above a whisper. "Maybe some water."

He nods and walks toward the gas station, leaving me under the flickering light. The silence feels heavier out here, away from the hum of the car. I glance at the horizon, where faint peaks of sunlight begin to break through, their glow blurred by the tears I've been holding back.

When he returns, he hands me a bottle of water, his eyes searching mine as though trying to uncover the truth I've been hiding. "You don't have to hide things from me, Mimi," he says softly. "Whatever it is, I'm here for you."

The lump in my throat swells, threatening to choke me, but I force a small smile. "I know, Dad. Thank you," I manage, though my voice trembles under the weight of my words.

We climb back into the car, and the road ahead stretches like an endless thread, unraveling toward something I can't avoid. The closer we get to home, the more I feel the walls I've built around myself start to crack, piece by piece.

The hum of the engine fills the silence between us, but it doesn't drown out the thoughts swirling in my mind. I glance at the window, watching the world blur by—trees swaying in the faint morning light, houses standing still as if time hasn't touched them. It feels like the world is holding its breath, waiting for me to face what I left behind.

Dad doesn't press me, doesn't speak, but I can feel his presence. His steady hands grip the wheel, his jaw set, and his eyes focused on the road ahead. It's the kind of silence I remember from long car rides as a kid, the kind where I could feel his concern without him saying a word.

I reach for the water bottle he handed me earlier, twisting the cap open. My throat feels dry, raw, as if every word I haven't said is stuck there. I take a sip and try to calm down before we get to the house.

"You'll like the changes I made to the house," he says suddenly, his voice breaking through the quiet. "I remodeled the kitchen. Finally got rid of that old wallpaper your mom loved so much."

I nod, giving a small smile. "The one with the flowers? You've been talking about getting rid of that since I was a kid."

"Yeah," he chuckles lightly, but there's an edge to his voice, like he's testing the waters for a deeper conversation.

I glance at him, noticing the way his knuckles tighten on the wheel. He wants to ask more, I can feel it, but he doesn't. Instead, he lets the silence settle again.

As we turn onto the familiar street, my chest tightens. The house comes into view, and I grip the water bottle in my lap a little harder. It looks the same, yet somehow different—painted a fresher white, the bushes trimmed neatly. The porch light is still on, though the sun has almost risen.

He pulls into the driveway, the tires crunching softly against the gravel. I stare at the house, memories rushing back like a wave threatening to pull me under. The fights with Mom, the nights I cried in my room, the moments I clung to Dad when I didn't know who else to turn to. It's all here, in this house, waiting for me.

Dad parks the car and shuts off the engine. For a moment, neither of us moves. The quiet feels deafening, the kind that fills your ears when you know something bad is about to happen.

"Home," he says softly, his voice both warm and uncertain. "It's been a while, huh?"

I nod, swallowing hard as I reach for the door handle. "Yeah. It has."

I step out of the car, the cool morning air hitting my face, sharp and sobering. I pull my coat tighter around me, watching as Dad grabs the bags from the trunk. My feet feel heavy as I take a few steps toward the porch, stopping just short of the first step.

The house looms ahead, familiar yet distant, like a dream I can't quite piece together. The windows seem to watch me, the door a silent witness to all the memories I left behind. The fights, the laughter, the quiet moments of peace—all of it lingers here, waiting for me to come back.

The silence stretches, broken only by the soft rustle of wind in the trees. I take a shaky breath, steeling myself to climb the steps, when the sound of the door creaking open freezes me in place.

I look up, and there she is.

Mom stands in the doorway, her figure framed by the soft glow of light spilling from inside. Her arms are crossed, her expression sharp. Her eyes meet mine, and for a moment, I can't breathe.

"You're finally here," she says, her voice low and cutting through the quiet like a blade.

I can't tell if it's anger or judgment in her tone—maybe both—but the weight of her presence is enough to hold me where I stand. My feet feel rooted to the gravel, the unspoken tension between us thick enough to drown in.

Dad steps closer, setting the bags down by the porch. "Let's go inside," he says gently.

But I can't move—not yet. I stand frozen, staring at the woman I've avoided for so long, the house behind her a shadow of everything I've been running from.

3.
Something Familiar

I close my eyes and let the memory creep back in. It's been three years, but the argument is still vivid, etched into my mind like a scar that refuses to fade.

"You're ruining your life, Reema! Running off with some boy? Is this what I raised you to be?" my mother's voice cuts through the still air of the house, sharp and unrelenting.

I whirl around, my chest heaving with frustration. "You didn't raise me! You controlled me, judged me—every single thing I did was wrong to you!"

Her face twists with anger, hands gesturing wildly like she's trying to grasp for words strong enough to express her fury. "Because I wanted what was best for you! And now, you're throwing it all away—for him? What do you even know about this boy?

My voice trembles, but I push through. "He's the first person who's ever made me feel like I'm enough! He loves me, supports me—something you've never done!"

Her dark eyes widen, and her voice rises, incredulous and biting. "Supports you? By taking you away from your family? From everything you've worked for? You think love is enough to make up for that? You're being foolish, Reema. You don't even see it."

"Foolish?" I shout, tears stinging my eyes. "Foolish is staying here and letting you suffocate me, letting you tear me down every time I try to live my life! Louvel believes in me, and I'd rather be with him than stay here and listen to you belittle me every day!"

My words strike like a slap, and for a moment, she is silent. But then she steps closer, her voice dropping to a low, cold fury. "Mark my words, Reema. One day, you'll see how wrong you are. You'll regret this. You'll regret leaving, throwing everything away for someone who doesn't deserve you. And when that day comes, don't you dare expect me to be waiting with open arms."

My breath catches as I fight the tears threatening to spill. I refuse to let her see me cry. Grabbing my bags with trembling hands, I turn toward the door.

At the doorway, I stop for a moment, taking everything in. Without looking back, I say, "I'll never regret leaving. I'll regret not doing it sooner."

Not waiting for a response, I storm out, slamming the door behind me. Louvel is by the car, leaning against it with his arms crossed, his expression unreadable. He doesn't say a word as I approach, simply opens the trunk and begins loading my bags.

I glance back at the house, catching a glimpse of her silhouette through the curtains, her arms crossed tightly. For a brief moment, guilt flickers in my chest, but it's quickly drowned out by anger. I climb into the car, slamming the door shut. Louvel slides into the driver's seat and starts the engine.

As we pull away, her figure grows smaller in the rearview mirror, her final words echoing in my mind. *"You'll regret this. One day, you'll realize how much you've thrown away."*

I stare straight ahead, my jaw set, hands clenched tightly in my lap. The tears never come. Anger fills every corner of me, leaving no room for anything else.

A voice pulls me out of the memory. "Come on," my father says gently.

I look up at him, nodding slightly. Taking a deep breath, I climb the steps to the porch. He holds the door open as I step inside. The familiar scent of pine cleaner and faint jasmine hits me instantly. My eyes scan the entryway, unchanged in three years—same faded rug, same slightly crooked family portrait on the wall.

She stands in the living room doorway, arms crossed, her sharp gaze cutting through me like a knife. My mother doesn't move closer, doesn't offer a smile or even a hint of welcome. Instead, her eyes roam over me.

"You look... tired," she says, her words steeped in judgment rather than concern.

I clench my jaw, forcing myself to take a steadying breath. "Hi, Mom. It's good to see you too."

Her lips thin, her expression unyielding. "I hope you're not planning to bring... all that baggage in here."

My father steps between us, his tone light but firm. "It's just a few bags, Salma. I'll take them to her room."

Her sharp gaze flicks to him, her lips tightening further. She doesn't argue, but she doesn't soften either. Instead, she turns away, walking into the living room. The tension in my shoulders eases slightly as I exhale.

"Come on, Mimi," my father says gently, motioning for me to follow him upstairs.

Trailing behind him, I climb the staircase. When we reach my old room, he pushes the door open and sets the bags near the bed.

"It's just as you left it," he says with a small, wistful smile. "Your mom hasn't touched a thing."

I glance around, taking it all in. Faded posters still hang on the walls, the bookshelf is crammed with my old novels, and the desk is cluttered with trinkets from a life that feels so far away. The bed, though stripped of its bedding, stands there like a quiet reminder of the person I used to be.

"Thanks, Dad," I say softly.

He turns to me, his expression tender. "I know it's not easy coming back. But I want you to know—you're always welcome here. No matter what."

I nod, my throat tightening. "I appreciate it," I manage, though my voice trembles.

He steps closer, placing a hand on my shoulder. "Take your time, Mimi. You've been through a lot. You don't have to face everything all at once."

The faintest smile tugs at my lips, a flicker of warmth in the heaviness that clings to me. "I'll try."

He gives my shoulder a gentle squeeze before stepping back. "I'll be downstairs if you need anything."

As he turns to leave, I call after him, my voice barely above a whisper. "Dad?"

He stops in the doorway, looking back.

"Thank you," I say, the weight of those two words hanging in the air.

He nods, his eyes soft with understanding. "Always."

When the door clicks shut behind him, the room falls silent. I sit on the edge of the bed, my hands resting in my lap. My mother's words replay in my mind, her disappointment as sharp and biting as ever. It's like being seventeen all over again, desperate to prove myself to a woman who always finds me lacking.

My gaze shifts to the window, sunlight streaming through the curtains. It softens the room, making it feel less suffocating. But even the light can't completely chase away the shadows that linger here, in this house and in me.

Downstairs, I can hear their voices, muffled. Dad's calm, measured tone. Mom's sharper, more critical replies. It's the same dynamic, the same tension that has always filled this house.

I lean back on the bed, letting out a shaky breath as my eyes wander around the room. It feels like stepping into a time capsule, a place frozen in the past, untouched by the chaos of the last three years. Everything is so familiar, yet I feel like a stranger here.

The posters on the wall catch my attention first. Bands I used to love, their faded colors reminding me of endless nights spent here with my headphones on, drowning out the world. My gaze shifts to the bookshelf, crammed with my old novels, some with dog-eared pages and others still pristine. How many nights did I escape into these stories, imagining lives far away from this house?

I push myself off the bed and walk toward the desk. My fingers brush against its surface, worn smooth from years of use. The memories hit me like a tidal wave—late nights spent sketching designs for photo shoots, writing down ideas for projects I never got to start. I run my hand along the edge, tracing the small nicks and scratches, each one a reminder of who I used to be.

I open one of the drawers hesitantly, the creak of the wood breaking the silence in the room. Inside, I find a stack of old photographs. My breath catches as I pick them up, thumbing through the images. There's a picture of the park where I first practiced photography, a black-and-white shot of my father laughing at something I can't remember, and even one of my mothers, her expression softer than I've seen in years. These were pieces of a life I once loved, a version of me that felt so far away now.

Digging deeper, my hand brushes against something solid and familiar. I pull out my old camera, the one my dad gave me for my thirteenth birthday. It feels heavier than I remember, or maybe I'm just more fragile now. I turn it over in my hands, running my fingers over the worn leather strap. The memories flood back—standing in the middle of the street to capture the perfect angle, sneaking photos of strangers at coffee shops, chasing sunsets just to see how they'd look through the lens.

I bring the camera up to my face instinctively, peering through the viewfinder. My finger hovers over the shutter button, but I don't press it. There's nothing here I want to capture, nothing I want to remember about this moment. Instead, I set it down gently on the desk, as if putting it to rest.

A sigh escapes me as I lean against the desk, staring at the scattered photographs. This room used to be my sanctuary, a place where I could dream, create, and escape. Now it feels like a museum exhibit—a collection of who I used to be before life caught up with me, before I made choices that led me so far from myself.

I pick up one of the photos again, the one of my fathers. He's laughing in it, carefree, his eyes crinkled with joy. I can almost hear his voice, calling me "Mimi" and telling me how proud he was of my work. A lump forms in my throat, and I clutch the photo tighter, as if it might anchor me to something real, something steady.

I shake my head and set the photo down, turning back toward the bed. As much as I want to lose myself in the nostalgia of this room, the weight of reality presses against me. I sit back down, folding my hands in my lap, and stare out the window.

The silence in the room grows heavier, wrapping around me like a blanket I can't shrug off. I glance back at the desk, at the camera and the photographs scattered across its surface. A part of me wants to pick it up again, to start over, to create something that feels like mine. But another part of me wonders if I'm too far gone—if the version of myself who dreamed big and captured beauty in the smallest moments is lost forever.

For now, I tell myself, this is enough. This room, this space, these fragments of who I was—they'll have to be enough. Maybe, just maybe, they'll help me find my way back.

4.
Fragile Foundations

I wake up to the soft glow of sunlight creeping through the curtains. For a moment, I forget where I am, the softness of the bed and the quietness of the room disorienting. Then it hits me—I'm home. I blink against the morning light, the ache in my body pulling me fully into reality. My muscles protest as I shift to sit up, the dull throbbing in my hips, thighs, and waist a painful reminder of everything I've been trying to push aside.

I swing my legs off the bed, my bare feet brushing against the familiar worn carpet. For a brief second, I want to bury myself back under the covers, pretend I'm a teenager again and that the last few years didn't happen. But the thought is fleeting, chased away by the weight of the bruises on my body and the soreness that lingers beneath my skin. I can't hide—not from myself, not anymore.

The first thing I do is head to the bathroom. The mirror above the sink reflects a version of myself I barely recognize. My makeup is smudged from falling asleep with it on, streaks of concealer and mascara staining my cheeks. My hair is a tangled mess, loose strands sticking to my neck and shoulders. But it's not the makeup or the disheveled hair that catches my attention—it's the bruising.

I lean closer to the mirror, tilting my head to examine the faint marks around my neck, where his hands had gripped me too tightly. My fingers hover over the darkened skin, not quite touching, as if confirming the bruises are real will make it worse. The shadows under my eyes are darker than I've ever seen, exhaustion etched into my face like a permanent fixture.

The sight of myself sends a pang of humiliation through me. How did I let it get this far? I splash cold water on my face, scrubbing away the remnants of makeup until the bruises are fully visible. There's no hiding it now—the marks on my body, the shadows in my eyes. I turn away from the mirror and start the shower, letting the steam rise around me before stepping in.

The hot water stings against the bruised and tender spots on my skin, but I don't flinch. I let it wash over me, gently washing my skin, as if I can cleanse myself of everything that happened. I close my eyes, and for a moment, I just stand there, letting the water mix with the tears I didn't realize I was crying.

Once the water begins to cool, I shut it off and step out, wrapping myself in a towel. I sit on the edge of the tub, running my fingers through my damp hair. My mind drifts to my nose, the way it bled so profusely that night. I tilt my head back and gently press along the bridge of it, wincing slightly. It's not broken—at least, I don't think so—but I know I need to see a doctor just to be sure.

After dressing in a loose shirt and sweatpants to avoid irritating the bruises, I make my way downstairs. The smell of coffee greets me, along with the sound of my dad humming faintly in the kitchen. For a moment, I feel a flicker of comfort, the familiarity of his presence grounding me. But then I hear my mom's voice—sharp, clipped, as if she's already found something to criticize. The warmth vanishes, replaced by a tightness in my chest.

I step into the kitchen, and they both look up. My dad offers me a soft smile, his eyes flicking to the bruises on my neck before quickly looking away. My mom, however, doesn't hide her reaction. Her gaze lingers, her lips pressing into a thin line.

"You should go to the doctor today," my mom says, her tone leaving no room for argument. Her gaze lingers on the bruises around my neck before shifting to my face. "And have them check your nose. That bruise on your neck looks awful, but your nose looks worse."

"It's not broken," I reply quietly, though my voice wavers. I touch my nose lightly, the tenderness making me flinch despite my words.

"Even if it's not broken, you should still have it looked at," my dad chimes in gently, setting a steaming mug of coffee in front of me. His voice is calm, but there's concern in his eyes as they flick briefly to my bruises. "It's better to be safe."

I nod, wrapping my hands around the mug as I stare into the dark liquid. I can feel my mom's eyes on me, heavy with judgment. The silence stretches, and I can almost hear the words she's biting back. My dad clears his throat, cutting through the tension.

"I can take you to the clinic this afternoon," he says, his tone light but firm. "We'll get it checked out."

"Okay," I mumble, my voice barely above a whisper.

The rest of the morning passes in a blur. My dad stays close, his presence steady and reassuring, while my mom busies herself with housework, occasionally throwing me sideways glances. I retreat to my room after breakfast, needing the solitude.

Back in my room, I sit on the edge of the bed. The photos I found last night are still scattered on my desk, along with my old camera. I pick up the camera again, running my fingers over the worn leather strap.

I lift it to my face, peering through the viewfinder. The familiar motion sends a pang of nostalgia through me. I snap a picture of the window, capturing the sunlight streaming through the curtains. It's nothing special, but it feels like a step—a small, hesitant step toward reclaiming something that used to be mine.

The click of the shutter echoes in the quiet room, and for the first time in what feels like days, I take a deep breath that doesn't feel forced. It's fragile, this moment, but it's mine.

I set the camera back on the desk, its weight still lingering in my hands like a tether to something I'm not sure I can hold onto anymore. My fingers hover over the photographs, tracing the edges of memories that feel both distant and achingly close. The picture of my dad laughing catches my eye again, his smile so genuine it almost feels like a stranger's face.

I pick it up, turning it over to see the faint handwriting on the back—my handwriting. "Summer, 2014. Dad's favorite joke about the barbecue." I chuckle under my breath, a sound so foreign that it startles me. He used to tell the worst jokes; the kind that made you groan and laugh all at once. I hadn't thought about them in years, but now, holding this photo, it feels like yesterday.

A knock at the door jolts me out of the memory. I quickly set the photo down, glancing toward the door. "Come in."

My dad steps in, his expression soft but serious. "You ready to head out? The clinic's not too far, but they close early today."

I nod, grabbing my bag and slinging it over my shoulder. "Yeah. Let's go."

We head downstairs, my mom lingering by the kitchen with her arms crossed. Her sharp gaze follows us as we walk past her. She doesn't say anything, but the tension in her posture speaks volumes. My dad places a hand on my shoulder as we step outside, his touch a quiet reassurance.

The drive to the clinic is quiet, the hum of the car filling the space between us. My dad doesn't push me to talk, and I'm grateful for that. The scenery blurs outside the window, a mix of familiar streets and unfamiliar storefronts. It's strange how much has changed in three years, yet some things feel exactly the same.

When we arrive, the clinic is almost empty, the faint smell of antiseptic greeting us as we step inside. The receptionist gives me a polite smile as my dad explains the situation. She hands me a clipboard with forms to fill out, and I sit down in the waiting area, the pen trembling slightly in my hand as I write my name.

I can feel my dad watching me, his quiet presence a comfort I didn't know I needed. When I finish the forms, he takes them back to the desk. Moments later, a nurse calls my name, and my stomach tightens as I stand up. My dad gives me an encouraging nod, but I don't look back as I follow the nurse down the hallway.

The exam room is cold, the kind of sterile cold that seeps into your bones. I sit on the edge of the examination table, my hands gripping the edge tightly. The nurse takes my vitals, her movements brisk and efficient.

She doesn't comment on the bruises, though her eyes linger on them for a moment too long.

When the doctor enters, he's a middle-aged man with kind eyes and a calm demeanor. "Reema, is it?" he asks, glancing at the clipboard. I nod, and he pulls up a stool, his gaze steady but nonjudgmental. "Let's take a look, shall we?"

I describe the injuries briefly, my voice clipped and detached. The doctor nods, his tone professional as he asks questions and examines my nose, pressing gently along the bridge. I flinch slightly at the tenderness, and he pulls back.

"It doesn't appear to be broken," he says, his voice reassuring. "There's some swelling and bruising, but structurally, everything looks intact. I'd recommend ice packs to reduce the swelling and over-the-counter pain relievers for any discomfort."

I nod, relief flooding through me despite the lingering ache. He moves on to the bruises around my neck, his gaze sharpening slightly. "These marks—did you have trouble breathing at any point?"

I hesitate, my fingers twisting the hem of my shirt. "No," I say finally, my voice barely above a whisper. "It wasn't... it wasn't that bad."

The doctor doesn't press further, though I can see the unspoken questions in his eyes. He hands me a pamphlet on treating bruises and another one I don't look at too closely before folding it into my bag. "If anything changes—difficulty breathing, increased pain—come back immediately," he says gently. I nod, muttering a quiet thank-you.

When I step back into the waiting room, my dad stands up immediately, his concern evident. "Everything okay?"

"Yeah," I reply, forcing a small smile. "Nothing's broken."

He exhales, relief softening his features. "Good. Let's get you home."

The drive back is quieter than the first, the weight of the doctor's questions lingering in my mind. I stare out the window, my fingers brushing over the pamphlets in my bag. One of them is about support resources, the kind meant for people in situations like mine. I know I should read it, but the thought of acknowledging what it implies feels too heavy right now.

When we pull into the driveway, my mom is waiting on the porch, her arms still crossed. My dad glances at me as we step out of the car, his expression unreadable. "Take a minute if you need to," he says, giving me a small, reassuring nod before heading up to the house.

As I climb the steps, my mom's gaze meets mine, sharp and probing. "Did they say anything about your nose?" she asks, her tone brisk.

"It's fine," I reply shortly, brushing past her and into the house. I don't wait for her response. Instead, I retreat to my room, closing the door behind me.

I sit down on the bed, the weight of the day settling over me like a heavy blanket. I pull out the pamphlet on bruises and read it carefully, letting the practical steps ground me. The other pamphlet stays folded in my bag, its presence a silent question I'm not ready to answer.

The instructions are straightforward: rest, apply cold compresses, and keep the bruised areas elevated if possible. I trace the lines of text with my finger, absorbing the words but feeling disconnected from them.

I set the pamphlet down and glance at my bag, the corner of the other pamphlet sticking out like it's taunting me. I know what it's about—the doctor's suggestion to seek counseling, to talk to someone about what I've been through. My dad had nodded encouragingly when the doctor handed it to me, but I'd stuffed it into my bag without a word. The idea of therapy feels overwhelming, like opening a door to everything I've been trying to avoid.

A soft knock at the door startles me. "Mimi, it's me," my dad says gently.

"Come in," I reply, my voice strained but steady.

He steps inside, carrying a cup of tea. He sets it down on the nightstand and sits on the edge of the bed, his presence warm and steady as always. "I wanted to check on you," he says, his eyes flicking briefly to the pamphlet on the bed. "I know today was a lot."

I nod, wrapping my hands around the mug. "Yeah... it was."

He hesitates for a moment, then says, "I know you don't want to talk about it yet, but... the doctor's suggestion about therapy—it's not a bad idea, Mimi. It might help."

I let out a shaky breath, staring into the tea as if it holds the answers. "I don't know if I can," I admit. "Talking about it... it feels too big. Like it'll swallow me whole."

His hand rests gently on my shoulder. "I get that," he says softly. "But you don't have to face it all at once. Therapy isn't about fixing everything overnight. It's about taking it one step at a time, at your own pace."

His words echo in my mind as I nod slowly, though I'm not sure if I'm agreeing or just trying to end the conversation. He seems to understand, patting my shoulder before standing up.

"Just think about it, okay?" he says before leaving the room.

The silence that follows feels heavier than before. I take a sip of the tea, its warmth spreading through me, but it doesn't ease the ache in my chest. I glance at the bag again, at the pamphlet sticking out. Slowly, reluctantly, I pull it out and unfold it. The words "Trauma Counseling" stare back at me, and for a moment, I feel like I can't breathe.

But then I remember my dad's voice: one step at a time, at your own pace. I set the pamphlet down on the nightstand, a small act of defiance against the fear gripping me. Maybe not today. But maybe soon.

The days blur together as I try to adjust to life back in my childhood home. My mom's presence is as sharp and cold as ever, her comments always just subtle enough to sting without leaving room for argument.

"You know, Reema, you could at least try to help around the house," she says one afternoon as I sit at the kitchen table, sorting through old photos. "It's not like you have much else going on."

I clench my jaw, forcing myself to take a deep breath before responding. "I'll help after I finish this," I say evenly, though the tension in my voice is hard to miss.

She doesn't respond, just huffs quietly and walks away. My dad catches my eye from across the room, giving me a small, apologetic smile. It's a silent reminder that he's on my side, even if he doesn't always intervene.

She doesn't say anything at first. Just crosses her arms and exhales through her nose, her eyes flicking over me like she's taking inventory of all my failures. She won't even meet my gaze. Her gaze lingers on the bruises peeking out from my collar, her lips pressing into a thin line as if to say, I told you so. It makes my skin crawl, but I bite my tongue. There's no point in arguing with her, not now.

A week passes, and I find myself settling into a fragile routine. I spend my mornings wandering through the house, rediscovering old memories in the trinkets and photos I'd left behind. My afternoons are quieter, spent sitting on the porch with my dad or taking long walks to clear my head. It's not much, but it feels like progress—like I'm slowly piecing myself back together.

One afternoon, as I sit on the porch steps, my dad joins me with a hesitant smile. "I called a counseling center," he says carefully. "Just to ask some questions. They said they have availability next week if you're interested."

I stare at the horizon, my heart racing. The thought of sitting in a room with a stranger, baring the pieces of myself I've kept hidden, feels suffocating. But my dad's expression is so hopeful, so full of quiet encouragement, that I find myself nodding.

"Okay," I say softly. "I'll go."

His smile widens, and he squeezes my hand. "I'm proud of you, Mimi."

After a few days of apprehension, I find myself sitting in Dr. Hayes's office for our first session. The space is warm and inviting, with soft, muted tones of cream and navy. A few plants line the windowsill, their leaves catching the light filtering through sheer curtains. The furniture is modern but not intimidating—a plush navy couch and two armchairs with wooden arms. Everything about this space feels intentional, from the neatly arranged bookshelves to the faint scent of lavender in the air.

Dr. Hayes sits across from me, her posture relaxed but attentive. She's wearing a navy blazer over a white blouse, paired with elegant gray trousers. Her light brown hair is swept into a messy bun, and her reading glasses rest on the bridge of her nose. Despite the professional attire, there's an ease about her, a warmth that puts me slightly at ease.

"Reema," she says, her voice steady and calm, with just the right amount of warmth. "It's nice to meet you. I know this first session can feel a bit overwhelming, so let's take it at your pace. How are you feeling today?"

I hesitate, my hands gripping the edge of the couch. "I don't know," I admit. "Nervous, I guess. I'm not really sure what I'm supposed to say."

Dr. Hayes nods, her expression gentle. "That's completely okay. There's no right or wrong way to start. This is your space, and my role is to support you. We can go as slowly as you need."

Her words are steady and reassuring, but I still feel a lump forming in my throat. I glance down at my hands, my fingers twisting the edge of my sleeve. "I guess... I don't really know where to begin. There's just so much, and it feels... messy."

"Life can feel that way sometimes," she says softly. "When things feel overwhelming, it can help to start with what's most present for you. What's been on your mind the most recently?"

I take a deep breath, my fingers tightening around my sleeve. "I left someone. Someone I've been with for a long time. He... he hurt me. A lot. And now I'm here, back at my parents' house, and everything feels... wrong. Like I don't know who I am anymore."

Her light blue eyes meet mine, and there's no judgment there, only quiet understanding. "Leaving a relationship like that takes incredible strength, Reema. It's not easy to walk away, especially when there's so much tied up in it—memories, emotions, even your sense of self."

I feel my throat tighten, and tears prickle at the corners of my eyes. "It doesn't feel strong," I whisper. "It feels... broken. Like I let it go on for too long. Like I should've seen the signs earlier."

Dr. Hayes leans forward slightly, her voice gentle but firm. "It's common to feel that way, but I want to remind you of something important: The responsibility for what happened lies with him, not you. Leaving was a brave step, and it's okay to feel conflicted. Healing takes time, and there's no timeline for when you're supposed to feel whole again."

Her words sink in slowly, like drops of water on parched soil. For the first time, I let myself consider the possibility that leaving Louvel wasn't just an escape—it was an act of courage, a step toward reclaiming myself.

Over the next few sessions, Dr. Hayes helps me start to untangle the web of emotions that's been choking me for years. We talk about Louvel—the way he made me feel seen and valued in the beginning, and how that shifted into control and manipulation. She helps me see patterns I hadn't noticed before, gently guiding me to connect the dots between my relationship with Louvel and the expectations I grew up with under my mother's watchful eye.

"Your mother's influence and Louvel's behavior aren't isolated," Dr. Hayes says during one session. "When someone grows up feeling judged or controlled, they can carry that dynamic into their relationships without realizing it. It doesn't mean you're at fault—it means those patterns became familiar, even if they weren't healthy."

The realization is like a punch to the gut, but it also makes sense. I've spent so much of my life trying to prove myself to people who never seemed satisfied—first my mother, then Louvel. The weight of that truth is overwhelming, but it's also freeing. I start to see the ways I've been carrying expectations that were never mine to bear.

One evening, after a particularly emotional session, I find myself back in my room, staring at my old camera. Dr. Hayes had encouraged me to reconnect with something that brought me joy before everything with Louvel. Photography used to be that for me, before it turned into a task I had to do. I hesitate, the camera feeling foreign in my hands, but eventually, I lift it to my face and snap a picture of the setting sun through my window.

The shutter clicks, and for the first time in a long time, I feel a flicker of something I can't quite name. It's small and fragile, but it's there—a reminder that I'm still here, still capable of finding beauty in the world.

5.
Knocking Past

A few weeks has gone by, I'm sorting through some of my old photographs when I hear the shouting. At first, I think it's just my parents arguing again—my mother criticizing something, and my dad trying to keep the peace. But then I catch a voice that doesn't belong in this house.

Louvel.

My stomach drops, a sickening wave of nausea rolling through me. I freeze, the photograph I'm holding slipping from my fingers. My dad's voice booms louder than I've ever heard, his usually calm demeanor shattered. He's shouting, something about "staying the hell away from my daughter."

I move toward the stairs, my heart pounding so hard it feels like it might burst through my chest. I reach the top step just as my dad's voice cuts through the air again.

"She doesn't want to see you! You've done enough damage, so get off my porch!"

"She's, *my* girlfriend! I have every right to talk to her!" Louvel shouts back, his voice dripping with desperation and anger. "You don't even know the whole story!"

I grip the railing to steady myself, my legs trembling. I can't see them yet, but I can picture the scene: my dad, his broad shoulders squared, towering over Louvel, who's probably putting on his usual act of self-righteousness. The door is half-open, and my mother's voice joins in.

"Of course he's here," she says. "You should've known this would happen. You invited this mess into your life, Reema."

Her words hit me like a slap, even though I'm not downstairs to hear the full force of them. I can feel the tears threatening, but I refuse to cry. Not now.

I take a deep breath and force myself to descend the stairs, one step at a time. When I round the corner, the sight before me is exactly what I imagined. My dad is standing in the doorway, his face red with fury, while Louvel stands just outside, his hands clenched into fists at his sides. My mom lingers in the background, her arms crossed, a scowl on her face.

Louvel's eyes find mine instantly. "Reema!" he calls, his voice softening. "Please. Just talk to me. I know I messed up, but we can fix this."

My dad steps further into the doorway, blocking Louvel's view. "She's got nothing to say to you," he growls. "And if you don't leave now, I'll call the police."

"You don't understand!" Louvel shouts, his composure slipping. "I love her! She loves me! You can't keep her locked up in this house forever!"

"Love?" My dad's voice rises, sharper than I've ever heard it. "You don't even know the meaning of the word! Love doesn't leave bruises on my daughter's neck or make her afraid to come home!"

Louvel flinches, his gaze flickering back to me. "Reema," he pleads, ignoring my dad entirely now. "Please, baby. Just let me explain. I'll—"

"No," I interrupt, my voice cutting through the chaos. It's small but firm, and everyone falls silent. Even my dad steps aside slightly, giving me space to face Louvel. My hands are trembling, but I ball them into fists, digging my nails into my palms to steady myself.

"No," I say again, louder this time. "I don't want to talk to you. I don't want to hear your excuses. Just go, Louvel."

He looks like I've slapped him, his jaw tightening as his expression shifts from pleading to anger. "You don't mean that," he says, shaking his head. "You're just saying that because they're here. They're poisoning you against me."

I laugh bitterly, though it feels more like a sob. "You think they're the problem? You think this is about them?" I step closer, ignoring the way my dad shifts protectively behind me. "You broke me, Louvel. You tore me down piece by piece until there was nothing left. And you want me to believe that's love?"

"Reema, I—" he starts, but I don't let him finish.

"Get out," I snap, my voice shaking with fury. "Get out, and don't come back. I'm done with you."

For a moment, he just stares at me, his expression unreadable. Then he mutters something under his breath, turning on his heel and storming off. I don't move until I hear the sound of his car peeling out of the driveway.

The silence that follows is deafening. My dad reaches out to touch my shoulder, but I pull away, my body still trembling. "I need a minute," I whisper, retreating back upstairs before anyone can stop me.

I don't make it far before my mom's voice follows me.

"Typical," she says, her tone laced with disdain. "You bring someone like that into your life, and this is what happens. I warned you, Reema. I told you he was no good."

I stop in my tracks, the rage bubbling up so quickly I can't control it. I spin around to face her, my vision blurred with tears. "You warned me?" I say, my voice shaking with fury. "What exactly did you warn me about, Mom? That I wasn't good enough? That no one would ever love me?"

She narrows her eyes, crossing her arms tighter. "Don't twist my words. You made your choice, Reema. You're the one who let him into your life."

"My choice?" I shout, my voice breaking. "You want to talk about choices? I chose him because I was desperate for someone—anyone—to love me! I chose him because you spent my entire life making me feel like I wasn't enough!"

Her face pales slightly, but she recovers quickly, her expression hardening. "Don't you dare blame me for this," she snaps. "I did everything I could for you—"

"You did everything you could to control me!" I cut her off, the words tumbling out before I can stop them. "You never supported me, never believed in me. All you cared about was making sure I lived up to your impossible standards. And when I didn't, you made sure I knew how much of a failure I was."

She opens her mouth to respond, but I don't let her.

"Louvel broke me," I say, voice barely holding. "In ways I don't have the words for. And you still want to stand there and tell me this was my fault?"

The silence that follows is suffocating. My mom stares at me, her mouth slightly open, but no words come out. For the first time, she looks... shaken.

"You didn't protect me," I whisper. "You didn't even see me. And now you want to act like you were right all along? Like this is what I deserve?"

Tears stream down my face, but I don't bother wiping them away. I take a step back, shaking my head. "I'm done trying to make you proud. I'm done letting you control me. You don't get to have power over me anymore."

I turn and walk away before she can say anything else, slamming my bedroom door behind me. My chest heaves with sobs as I collapse onto the bed, the weight of everything crashing down on me.

Later that night, the knock at my door is soft, almost hesitant, but I hear it clearly in the quiet of my room.

"Mimi?" My dad's voice follows, gentle and patient.

"I'm proud of you," he says after a long silence. "For standing up to him. And to her."

"Come in," I manage, my voice shaky. I've been sitting on the edge of my bed, staring at the photos scattered across my desk, trying to make sense of everything swirling in my head.

He steps inside, closing the door quietly behind him. He doesn't sit right away, instead hovering near the dresser, his hands in his pockets.

The way his shoulders are slightly hunched, the furrow in his brow—it's like he's carrying the weight of my pain along with his own.

"You don't have to talk if you're not ready," he says after a moment, his voice soft but steady. "I just wanted to check on you."

I look up at him, and something in his expression—a mix of worry and quiet encouragement—makes the dam crack. I feel the tears welling up again, but this time, I don't try to stop them. "I think I need to talk," I say, my voice trembling. "I just... I don't know where to start."

He nods, stepping closer and sitting on the edge of the bed next to me. He doesn't rush me, doesn't press. He just waits, his presence steady and safe, like he's bracing himself for whatever I'm about to say.

I draw in a shaky breath, staring at my hands twisting the blanket in my lap. "Dad," I start, my voice barely above a whisper, "I called you that night because I didn't know where else to go. I didn't think you'd even pick up. It had been so long, and I... I wasn't sure if you'd want to hear from me."

His expression shifts, pain flickering across his face. "Mimi," he says softly, his voice breaking. "I'll always pick up for you. Always."

I nod, swallowing hard as I try to find the words. "I left because I couldn't take it anymore. The way he treated me... it was killing me. He made me feel like I was nothing. Like I couldn't live without him. And for a long time, I believed him."

My voice cracks, and the dam bursts. The words pour out, spilling over each other in a rush of emotion. "He controlled everything—what I wore, who I talked to, where I went. He'd get so mad if I didn't answer my phone right away or if I spent too long at work. It was—" My breath catches, and I press a hand to my chest, trying to calm the storm inside me. "It was hitting, grabbing, throwing things. It didn't matter what I said or did. It was never enough."

My dad's hands tighten into fists, his knuckles white, but he doesn't interrupt. His jaw is clenched, and his eyes glisten with unshed tears.

"And that night..." My voice breaks, and I wipe at my cheeks, the tears falling faster now. "That night, I swore he broke my nose. He said it wasn't broken, but it was bleeding so much, and I—I didn't know what to do. He kept blaming me, saying I pushed him to it. And then..." I pause, the words catching in my throat. "He—he did things. Things I—I can't explain."

My dad's face crumples, and a tear slips down his cheek. "Mimi," he whispers, his voice thick with emotion. "I—"

"I wanted to leave so many times," I interrupt, my words tumbling out in a rush. "But every time, he'd promise to change. He'd say he loved me, that he was sorry, and I wanted to believe him so badly. I thought maybe if I was better, if I just tried harder, he wouldn't hurt me anymore. But it never stopped, Dad. It never stopped."

My hands tremble as I wipe at my face, my chest heaving with sobs. "And tonight, when he showed up here, all I could think was, 'What if he doesn't leave? What if he doesn't stop?'" I look up at my dad, my eyes pleading. "I was so scared, Dad. I didn't know what to do."

He reaches for me then, pulling me into his arms. His embrace is tight, almost desperate, as if he's trying to hold all the broken pieces of me together. "Mimi," he whispers, his voice shaking. "I'm so sorry. I'm so, so sorry."

I bury my face in his shoulder, the warmth of his hug making me feel small and safe all at once. "It's not your fault," I choke out. "I didn't tell you. I didn't tell anyone. I thought I could handle it. I thought I could fix it."

"You shouldn't have had to handle it," he says fiercely, pulling back just enough to look me in the eyes. His face is a mix of anger, sadness, and relief. "He had no right to do those things to you. None. And if I had known—if I'd even suspected—I would've done everything in my power to stop it. To protect you."

The tears streaming down his face mirror my own, and for the first time in years, I see just how deeply he feels my pain. "I hate that he hurt you," he says, his voice trembling with anger. "I hate that he made you feel like you had no way out. But you're out now, Mimi. You're here. And you're safe. He'll never hurt you again—I'll make sure of it."

I nod, my tears soaking into his shirt as I cling to him. "I'm so tired," I whisper.

His arms tighten around me, his voice steady despite the emotion in it. "I know, sweetheart. I know. But you don't have to do this alone anymore. I'm here. We'll get through this together, one step at a time."

For a long moment, we sit there, holding onto each other as the weight of everything I've been carrying starts to lift. It's not gone—not even close—but it feels a little lighter, knowing I don't have to carry it alone anymore.

6.
Healing Ties

The next morning, I wake up with swollen eyes and a heavy heart, but there's a flicker of something else—a small, fragile sense of relief. My dad's words from the night before echo in my mind: *You're out now. You're safe. He'll never hurt you again.*

I sit up in bed, rubbing at my temples as the sunlight streams through the curtains. The events of the previous night replay in my head—Louvel's voice on the porch, my dad's anger, my mother's cutting words, and finally, the dam breaking as I told my dad everything. The yelling was gone now, but the air still felt cracked. My chest ached from holding my breath too long, and the house was too still—like the silence was waiting for someone to break it again.

My phone sits on the nightstand, the therapist's pamphlet next to it. For days, I've been staring at the number, unwilling to call, unsure if I could face the conversation waiting on the other end. But now, as I pick it up and scroll through my contacts, I feel an urgency—like if I don't call now, I'll lose this sliver of courage.

I press the call button, and Dr. Hayes answers on the third ring, her calm voice instantly putting me at ease.

"Hello, Reema. It's good to hear from you."

"I—" My voice falters, and I take a shaky breath. "I need to talk. About everything."

There's a brief pause before she responds, her tone gentle and steady. "I'm here to listen, Reema. Take your time."

For the next half hour, I pour everything out—the details I hadn't shared in our earlier sessions, the depths of what Louvel did to me, the fear and shame that kept me silent for so long. I tell her about the night I left, the bruises, the desperation, and the guilt that still clings to me like a second skin. And as I speak, I feel the weight begin to shift, as if the words themselves are lifting pieces of it away.

"You've shown so much strength, Reema," Dr. Hayes says when I finish, her voice warm with admiration. "Facing this, talking about it—it's an incredible step forward. And you did it. You survived."

I blink back tears, her words settling deep in my chest. "It doesn't feel strong," I admit. "It feels... like I'm still broken."

"Healing isn't a straight line," she reminds me gently. "It's messy, and it's hard, but every step you take—no matter how small—is progress. I want you to focus on reconnecting with the parts of yourself that bring you joy, the things that make you feel whole. You've spent so much time surviving; now it's time to start living again."

Her words stay with me long after the call ends. I sit on the edge of the bed, staring at the scattered photographs on my desk. Slowly, I reach for my camera, the weight of it familiar and grounding in my hands. Dr. Hayes is right—I need to find myself again. And maybe this is where I start.

The next few days are a blur of tentative steps forward. I start small—taking walks around the neighborhood, snapping pictures of the familiar streets and parks I used to visit as a teenager. Each click of the shutter feels like reclaiming a piece of myself, a quiet defiance against the darkness that tried to consume me.

I find myself drawn to places I used to love, places that hold echoes of who I was before Louvel. The old library downtown, with its towering shelves and dusty sunbeams. The small park by the river, where I spent hours as a teenager capturing the way light danced on the water's surface.

One afternoon, I decide to visit the local coffee shop where I used to spend hours studying and sketching. As I step inside, the warm scent of freshly brewed coffee wraps around me like a comforting embrace. I order my drink and take a seat by the window, pulling out my camera to review the photos I've taken over the past few days.

As I sift through the photos, I feel a strange mix of emotions—nostalgia, sadness, and a flicker of hope. It's not perfect, and it's not easy, but for the first time in years, I feel like I'm taking steps toward something real.

"Reema?"

The voice is hesitant but unmistakable, and my heart skips a beat. I look up to see Asmin standing a few feet away, her wide, dark eyes filled with surprise. She looks almost the same as I remember—her curly hair pulled into a loose ponytail; her smile hesitant but warm.

"Asmin," I breathe, my voice barely above a whisper.

She takes a step closer, her expression shifting from surprise to something softer, tinged with sadness. "I can't believe it's really you. It's been... so long."

I nod, my throat tightening. "It has. Too long."

She sits down across from me, her hands fidgeting with the strap of her bag. "I didn't know you were back. I thought—" She pauses, searching for the right words. "I thought you forgot about me."

Guilt washes over me, and I lower my gaze. "I didn't forget," I say quietly. "I just... I didn't know how to reach out. Everything got so complicated, and I—"

"It's okay," she interrupts gently, her smile tinged with sadness. "I was hurt, yeah, but I always figured you had your reasons. I just... I missed you."

Her words hit me harder than I expect, and I feel the tears welling up again. "I missed you too," I whisper. "More than I can say."

We talk for a while, catching up on what's happened over the past couple years. We talk about our careers first; I tell her all about my photography and where I've gotten. But then the conversation switches, we start to talk about Louvel. I catch her watching me carefully, her eyes filled with a mix of warmth and pain. "You don't have to explain everything," she says, her voice soft. "But if you want to, I'm here."

I hesitate, unsure where to begin, but Asmin's steady gaze makes it easier to let the words flow. "It wasn't always bad," I start, my voice shaking. "At first, he was... perfect. Or I thought he was. But then, little by little, he changed. And I didn't realize how bad it was until I couldn't leave."

Her expression shifts, her lips pressing into a thin line. "What did he do to you, Reema?"

The question hangs in the air, and for a moment, I'm sixteen again, sitting on Asmin's bed after a fight with my mom, tears streaming down my face as I told her, *"I'm not good enough for her."* Back then, she held my hand and told me, *"You're good enough for me, and that's all that matters."*

Now, her voice pulls me back to the present, steady and unwavering. "Reema, you don't have to carry this alone. You never did."

"I didn't mean to shut you out," I say, my voice cracking. "I was ashamed, and I thought if I told you, you'd think less of me."

"Less of you?" Her voice rises, her dark eyes blazing with anger—not at me, but for me. "Reema, do you have any idea how much I care about you? How much it hurt not knowing where you were? I don't care how messy things got. I would've been there."

I swallow hard, tears slipping down my cheeks. "I know that now," I whisper. "I just... I couldn't see it then."

Asmin reaches into her bag and pulls out an old photo—one of us sitting by the river, laughing so hard we're clutching our stomachs. "You gave this to me the night before you left," she says softly. "I kept it on my mirror for years, hoping you'd come back. And now you're here."

I take the photo from her, my fingers brushing the worn edges.

As we leave the coffee shop, the sun is setting, painting the streets in golden light. Asmin walks beside me, her arm brushing mine.

"I don't care how long it's been," she says, her voice firm. "You're my best friend, Reema. We're going to fix this."

I glance at her, my heart swelling with gratitude. "I'd like that," I say quietly.

She smiles, the kind of smile that feels like home.

I look at her in admiration, then a thought comes to mind: *I've found a piece of myself again.*

7.
Kindling Light

It wasn't planned, running into Lila again. It had only been a few months since I last saw her, back when I had stumbled into the hotel after leaving Louvel, broken and unsure of where to go. She had been kind to me then, offering tissues and a warm smile without asking for more than I could give. I hadn't expected to see her again, but there she was.

I had been walking the city with my camera, capturing the familiar streets and hidden corners I'd rediscovered in the time since I left Louvel. When the hotel came into view, I stopped, drawn by a pull I couldn't explain. Lifting my camera, I focused on the way the sunlight hit the brick façade, the small details I hadn't noticed before.

"Reema?"

Her voice startled me, and I lowered the camera quickly. Turning, I saw her standing a few feet away, her hands clutching a notepad and pen. Her uniform was neat, but her hair was slightly mussed, like she had been rushing around all day. And yet, her amber eyes still held that warmth I remembered.

"Lila," I said, surprised but unable to keep the smile off my face. "Hi."

She returned the smile, though hers was softer, tinged with something I couldn't place. "Hi," she said. "I didn't think I'd see you again. How've you been?"

I hesitated for a moment, then shrugged. "Better. Figuring things out, one step at a time."

Her smile grew. "That's good to hear. I've been thinking about you, you know. Wondering how you were doing."

That admission made my heart skip a beat. "Really?"

"Of course," she said, her gaze unwavering. "You kind of left an impression."

For a moment, I was too stunned to respond. I had spent so much time feeling like a ghost of myself that the idea of leaving any kind of impression on someone felt foreign. "Well... here I am," I finally said, gesturing toward the hotel.

She laughed softly, the sound like a balm to my frayed nerves. "Yeah, here you are. Taking photos, I, see?"

I nodded, holding up my camera. "It's... therapeutic."

Her expression softened further, and she gestured toward a bench near the hotel's garden. "Do you have a few minutes? I'd love to catch up. I never got to know your story."

I hesitated, nervousness bubbling up, but her gaze was so open, so genuine, that it was impossible to say no. "Yeah, sure."

We sat down, the sounds of the city fading into the background as we talked. I told her about my photography, about how it had become my lifeline in the months since I left my ex Louvel. She listened intently, her questions thoughtful, her presence grounding. When I asked about her, she shared stories about her family, her dreams of traveling, and how much she loved working at the hotel—even if it was chaotic at times.

Time seemed to melt away as we talked, the conversation flowing as naturally as if no time had passed since we first met. The way she looked at me, her amber eyes full of quiet understanding, made something deep inside me shift.

As the sun dipped lower in the sky, casting a warm glow over the garden, I found myself feeling bold. I hesitated for a moment, but then I reminded myself of everything I had survived. This was my chance to start fresh, to take a step toward something good.

"Lila," I began, my voice steady despite the nerves bubbling in my chest. She tilted her head slightly, her expression curious. "Would you... want to grab dinner with me sometime? As, um, a date?"

Her eyes widened slightly, and for a brief moment, I thought I had made a mistake. But then her smile grew, soft and radiant, and she nodded. "I thought you'd never ask."

Relief and something close to excitement swirled in my chest, and I couldn't help but laugh. "So, that's a, yes?"

"It's definitely a yes," she said, her gaze warm and steady.

Time went on after our first date, the nights with Lila started to feel like the world was holding its breath, like the city outside was quiet just for us. We've carved out a space that feels untouched by the noise and chaos, a cocoon where only our truths exist. Late at night, when no one is around, we talk about everything—our fears, our regrets, the wounds we carry. Her words are a salve, her voice soft but unwavering, and I find myself telling her things I've never told anyone.

One night, we're lying on her living room floor, the glow of candles flickering around us. The room smells faintly of lavender, her favorite scent, and her hand rests lightly on mine. The silence between us is comfortable, but I feel the pull to say something I've been holding back for years.

"Lila," I begin, my voice barely above a whisper. "There's something I haven't told you."

She turns her head to look at me, her amber eyes steady and kind. "You can tell me anything," she says, her thumb brushing gently against my knuckles.

I take a deep breath, my chest tightening. "It's about... my family. My mom." My voice catches, and I hesitate. "And me."

Her expression doesn't change—there's no shock, no pity, just a quiet invitation for me to continue. It's the steadiness in her gaze that gives me the courage to speak.

"My mom's... devout. You know? She's always been religious. Growing up, it felt like everything I did was being weighed, judged. There were rules for how to dress, how to speak, how to act. Who to love." My voice wavers on that last word, and I swallow hard.

"She caught me with a boy when I was in high school," I say, my voice shaking. "It wasn't even anything serious. We were just... kissing. But to her, it was the end of the world. She said I'd dishonored the family.

That I'd tainted myself. She called me a disgrace. And then—" My voice cracks, and I close my eyes, tears slipping down my cheeks. "She hit me. Over and over. Like she could beat the shame out of me."

Lila's hand tightens around mine, grounding me, but she doesn't interrupt. She lets me keep going.

"That was bad enough," I whisper, "but I knew... I knew even then that wasn't the whole truth. The boy—he wasn't the only one. I liked girls too. I always have. And if she found out..." My words falter, my throat tightening around the weight of my fear. "I don't know what she'd do."

I turn my face away, ashamed. "Even now, I can hear her voice in my head. Telling me I'm wrong, that I'm sinful, that I'm going to hell. And sometimes... sometimes I believe her."

Lila shifts closer, her hand cupping my cheek, gently guiding me to face her. Her touch is soft but firm, her gaze unwavering. "Reema," she says, her voice steady but filled with emotion. "You are not wrong. You are not sinful. And you are definitely not going to hell. Who you are—every part of you—is beautiful. And anyone who can't see that doesn't deserve to have you in their life."

Tears spill over, and I shake my head. "But she's, my mom. She's supposed to love me. I want to believe she would, but I'm so scared she won't. And it's not just her—what will my family think? What will they say? How can I face them knowing they might never look at me the same way again?"

Her thumb brushes away my tears, her touch soothing. "You don't have to face them alone," she says softly. "I'm here. And no matter what happens, no matter what anyone says, you have me. And I will remind you every day that you are enough."

Her words crack something open inside me, and the sobs come hard and fast, shaking my entire body. Lila pulls me into her arms, holding me tightly, her presence anchoring me as I let out years of pain and fear. Her hands stroke my back in slow, comforting circles, and she murmurs soft reassurances into my ear.

When my tears finally subside, I pull back slightly, just enough to meet her gaze. "How do you do that?" I ask, my voice hoarse. "How do you always know exactly what to say?"

She smiles gently, brushing a strand of hair from my face. "Because I see you, Reema. All of you. And I care about you—all of you."

Her words settle into the deepest corners of my heart, filling spaces I didn't even know were empty. I lean into her touch, the warmth of her hand against my cheek grounding me in a way I've never experienced before.

"Thank you," I whisper. "For being here."

Her smile softens, and she presses her forehead against mine. "Always," she says. "Always."

Our late-night conversations become a ritual, a sacred space where nothing is off-limits. One night, as we lie on the couch, her head resting on my chest, she asks me about my photography.

"Why do you love it so much?" she murmurs, her fingers tracing lazy patterns on my arm.

I think about her question for a moment before answering. "It's the way it makes me feel. When I'm behind the camera, it's like I can see the world differently—like I'm capturing moments that might otherwise go unnoticed. It's... grounding."

She lifts her head to look at me, her expression thoughtful. "Do you think it's because you're trying to find pieces of yourself in those moments?"

Her question catches me off guard, but as I consider it, I realize she might be right. "Maybe," I admit. "Maybe I'm looking for something I lost a long time ago."

She nods, her gaze soft. "I think you're finding it," she says, her voice filled with quiet faith. "Piece by piece, frame by frame. And I think you're stronger than you give yourself credit for."

Her belief in me feels like a lifeline, and I find myself reaching for her hand, holding it tightly. "You make me feel like I can do anything," I say, my voice barely above a whisper.

She smiles, her eyes shimmering with emotion. "That's because you can."

The intimacy between us grows in quiet, unspoken ways. It's in the way she touches me—lightly, reverently, as if she's afraid of breaking me but determined to show me I'm whole. It's in the way she looks at me, like I'm the only person in the room, the only person who matters.

One evening, as we sit on her balcony, she asks me about my dreams.

"If you could do anything, without fear or doubt, what would it be?" she asks, her voice soft but insistent.

I hesitate, the question unfamiliar and daunting. "I don't know," I admit. "I've spent so long trying to survive, I don't think I've ever let myself dream."

She reaches for my hand, her touch grounding. "Then maybe it's time to start," she says. "And I'll be here to remind you that you deserve every dream you have."

Her words settle into the corners of my heart, and for the first time in years, I allow myself to imagine a future—a future where I'm not defined by my past, where I'm free to be myself, fully and unapologetically.

The night she tells me she loves me, it's quiet and unassuming, but it feels monumental.

We're lying in bed, the moonlight spilling through the window. Her fingers gently brushing my chest like a brush to a canvas, and her voice is barely above a whisper when she says, "I love you, Reema."

The words catch me off guard, and for a moment, I don't know how to respond. But then I look at her—the vulnerability in her eyes, the quiet strength in her expression—and I realize I feel the same.

"I love you too," I say, my voice trembling with emotion. "I think I've loved you since the moment you gave me that tissue in the lobby."

She laughs softly, her eyes glistening. "Then it's a good thing I worked at that hotel."

The night with Lila unfolds in quiet intimacy. The soft glow of the moonlight through the window outlines her face, and I can't look away. Her fingers trail lightly up my arm, leaving a shiver in their wake. We're lying tangled on her bed, the world outside forgotten. She leans in, her lips brushing against my neck, soft and deliberate, igniting sparks that run down my spine.

Her voice is low, barely a whisper. "Do you know how beautiful you are?"

I tilt my head, giving her access, my breath catching as she presses another kiss just below my jawline. "You don't have to say that," I murmur, though my voice betrays how much her words affect me.

"I don't have to," she says, her lips slipping over my collarbone now. "But I mean it. Every word."

Her hand finds my waist, her touch both grounding and electrifying. My own hands hesitate for a moment before sliding up her back, feeling the warmth of her skin beneath my fingertips. She sighs into me, her breath warm against my ear, and I close my eyes, letting the moment consume me.

Her lips return to my neck, her teeth grazing just enough to leave a faint, tingling sensation. A soft gasp escapes me, and I feel her smile against my skin. "I love that sound," she says, her voice laced with amusement and desire.

I open my eyes, meeting hers in the dim light. "You're impossible," I say, though the smile on my face betrays my words.

"And yet, here you are," she teases, her fingers slipping beneath the hem of my shirt, tracing patterns on my skin. "With me."

My heart pounds in my chest as she leans in again, her lips capturing mine this time. The kiss is slow and tender, deepening as her hand moves to cup my cheek. It's not just physical—it's everything we've been building between us, all the unspoken words and fragile emotions laid bare. When we finally pull back, her forehead rests against mine, her breath mingling with mine in the stillness of the room.

"You make me feel..." I pause, searching for the right words. "Like I'm alive again."

She smiles, her thumb brushing over my cheek. "That's all I want—to see you happy."

I pull her closer, letting the moment stretch on, her warmth and love wrapping around me like a shield against the world.

8.
Embracing Change

The morning sunlight spills through the curtains, bathing the living room in a soft golden glow. I'm on cloud nine as I walk up the path to my house, the warmth of Lila's goodbye kiss lingering on my skin. I can still feel the faint imprint of her lips on my neck from the night before, a subtle reminder of our time together. My fingers brush over the spot absently as I reach the door, a small, content smile tugging at my lips.

The moment I step inside, though, the air shifts. My mother's voice cuts through the stillness like a whip.

"Out all night again?" she snaps, her arms crossed as she stands in the kitchen doorway. "What exactly are you doing, Reema? Wandering the streets like some stray?"

My mood plummets, her words like cold water dousing the warmth in my chest. "I wasn't wandering the streets," I say evenly, trying to keep my tone neutral. "I was with a friend."

Her eyes narrow, her lips curling in disdain. "A friend," she repeats, her voice dripping with sarcasm. "Don't insult my intelligence. I saw the mark on your neck. Do you think I'm blind?"

My cheeks flush, but I don't back down. "It's none of your business," I say firmly, stepping past her toward the stairs.

She follows, her voice rising. "None of my business? You live under my roof, young lady. Everything you do is my business. And if you think for one second, I'll tolerate this—this disgusting behavior—you're sorely mistaken."

I stop in my tracks, my hands balling into fists at my sides. "Disgusting behavior?" I repeat, turning to face her. "Loving someone—being happy—is disgusting to you?"

Her face twists in anger, but before she can respond, my dad's voice cuts through the tension.

"Salma, enough!" His tone is sharp, louder than I've ever heard it, and it startles both of us. He steps into the room, his face set in a rare expression of anger. "I'm tired of this. Every time she walks through that door, you're waiting to pounce on her. You're driving her away."

My mother's mouth opens and closes, her usual composure faltering. "I'm trying to protect her," she says finally, her voice defensive. "She's throwing her life away with—"

"With what?" my dad interrupts, his voice rising. "With someone who makes her happy? With someone who actually treats her with kindness and respect? You want to talk about throwing lives away? Let's talk about how you've spent years tearing her down!"

Her face pales, but she recovers quickly, her expression hardening. "I'm her mother. It's my job to teach her right from wrong."

"And you think this is how you do it?" he snaps, his voice trembling with anger. "By shaming her for who she is? For who she loves? She's not wrong, Salma. She's not broken. But if you keep this up, you're going to lose her for good."

"You're exaggerating," she hisses, her arms crossing tighter over her chest. "I have every right to be concerned. Look at the mess she's made of her life. Louvel—"

My dad cuts her off again, his voice booming. "Louvel? Louvel? Are you really going to stand here and blame her for what he did? That boy is a monster, and you know it! Reema didn't ask to be abused. She didn't ask for any of what happened to her. But instead of supporting her, you've spent every waking moment making her feel like it's her fault."

My mother flinches, but she doesn't back down. "I didn't say it was her fault," she snaps, though her voice wavers. "But she made choices, and—"

"She made choices because she's human, Salma!" he roars, his fists clenching at his sides. "She made choices because she's trying to find her way in a world that hasn't exactly been kind to her. And instead of being her anchor, you've been another storm."

The words hang heavy in the air, and for the first time, I see the cracks in my mother's armor. Her lips press into a thin line, but she says nothing.

My dad turns to me then, his expression softening. "Reema," he says gently, "I'm sorry. I should've spoken up sooner. I should've defended you a long time ago, but I won't stand by and let this continue. Not anymore."

Tears sting my eyes as I watch him, his words hitting me harder than I expected. He looks back at my mom, his voice steady but firm. "She's our daughter, Salma. And whether you like it or not, she deserves to be happy. If that means being a photographer, then so be it. If that means having a girlfriend, then so be it. She's not here to live up to your expectations—she's here to live her life."

My mom's face twists, a mix of hurt and anger flashing across her features. "And what about her soul?" she demands, her voice trembling. "What about everything we taught her—everything we believe in?"

"What good are beliefs," my dad counters, his voice rising again, "if they make you incapable of loving your own child?"

The silence that follows is deafening. My mother's face crumples, and for a moment, I think she might say something, but she just turns and walks away, disappearing into the kitchen.

My dad exhales deeply, running a hand through his hair. He turns back to me, his shoulders slumping slightly. "Are you okay?" he asks softly.

I nod, though my throat feels tight. "Thank you," I whisper. "For standing up for me."

He steps closer, placing a hand on my shoulder. "You don't have to thank me, Mimi," he says softly. "I'm your father, I should've done it a long time ago."

His words bring fresh tears to my eyes, but this time, they're tears of relief. For the first time in years, I feel seen—truly seen—and it's enough to crack something open inside me.

"I love you, Dad," I whisper, my voice trembling.

He pulls me into a tight hug, his hand cradling the back of my head like he used to when I was a child. "I love you too, sweetheart," he says, his voice thick with emotion. "And I'm so damn proud of you. For everything."

"So," my dad begins, his tone lighter now, "this friend of yours." He gives me a knowing smile, his eyebrows quirking just slightly.

I blush, fiddling with the hem of my sleeve. "She's... more than a friend," I admit, my voice barely above a whisper.

He nods, his expression softening. "I figured," he says gently. "She's the one who put that smile on your face this morning, isn't she?"

I can't help but grin, my cheeks warming. "Yeah. Her name's Lila."

"Lila," he repeats, as if trying the name out. "She must be pretty special."

"She is," I say, unable to keep the emotion from my voice. "She's... everything. She makes me feel like I can be myself. Like I don't have to hide or apologize for who I am."

My dad leans forward, resting his elbows on his knees. "That's all I've ever wanted for you, Mimi," he says softly. "Someone who sees you, who loves you for who you are—not who they want you to be."

I look at him, the lump in my throat growing. "Would you want to meet her?" I ask hesitantly. "I mean, if you're okay with it."

His face lights up with a smile that takes me by surprise. "I'd love to meet her," he says warmly. "If she's as wonderful as you say, I'd like to see this person who's treating my daughter the way she deserves."

The relief that floods through me is overwhelming. "Really?" I ask, my voice trembling slightly.

"Really," he says firmly. "Invite her over. Whenever she's free."

I don't waste a moment, pulling out my phone to text Lila. She responds almost immediately, her excitement palpable even through the screen. Within an hour, she's at the door, her nervous smile turning into a radiant grin when she sees me.

"Hi," she says softly, leaning in to kiss my cheek. "You ready?"

I nod, squeezing her hand before leading her inside. My dad stands as we enter the living room, his demeanor warm and welcoming.

"Lila," I say, my voice steady despite the butterflies in my stomach, "this is my dad. Dad, this is Lila."

"It's so nice to meet you, sir," Lila says, extending her hand. Her voice is confident but kind, and I can tell she's making an effort to leave a good impression.

My dad shakes her hand, his grip firm but not intimidating. "Call me William," he says, his smile genuine. "And it's nice to meet you too, Lila. Reema's told me a lot about you."

Lila glances at me, her cheeks pinking slightly. "All good things, I hope."

"Only good things," he assures her, gesturing for her to sit. As we settle onto the couch, the conversation flows more easily than I expected. My dad asks Lila about her work, her interests, and her family, and she answers with a mix of humor and sincerity that quickly puts him at ease.

But it's when she talks about me that my heart feels like it might burst.

"She's incredible, you know," Lila says, her gaze flickering to mine. "Her photography—it's more than just pictures. It's like she captures the soul of a moment, the way it feels, not just the way it looks. I keep telling her she needs to share it with the world, but she's stubborn."

I laugh, rolling my eyes. "I'm not stubborn. I'm... cautious."

"Scared of what?" my dad asks, his tone curious rather than critical.

I shift uncomfortably, running a hand through my hair. "Of failing, I guess," I admit. "Of putting myself out there and not being good enough."

My dad leans forward, his expression serious. "Mimi, your talent is a gift. And gifts are meant to be shared. You've spent so much time doubting yourself, but you're stronger than you realize. And you're not alone in this. You've got people who believe in you—Lila, me, and probably more than you think."

Lila reaches for my hand, her touch grounding. "You don't have to do it all at once," she says softly. "But taking that first step—it's worth it. You're worth it."

The sincerity in their voices, the warmth in their eyes—it's enough to melt the last of my resistance. I nod slowly, a small but genuine smile tugging at my lips. "Okay," I say quietly. "I'll do it. I'll submit my work to the gallery."

The relief and pride in their faces are palpable, and for the first time in a long time, I feel like I'm standing on solid ground.

That night, after the submission email is sent and the weight of the day begins to lift, I find myself back at Lila's apartment. The city hums quietly outside her window, and the soft glow of candlelight casts the room in a warm, golden hue.

She pulls me into her arms, her fingers trailing lightly along my spine as she presses a gentle kiss to my forehead. "I'm proud of you," she whispers, her lips brushing against my skin. "For being brave. For letting yourself shine."

Her words send a shiver down my spine, and I tilt my head to meet her gaze. Her eyes are warm and full of love, and I can't help but lean in, capturing her lips in a kiss that's soft and slow and full of promise.

Her hands find my waist, pulling me closer as her lips move to my neck, her touch both gentle and insistent. My breath catches as she murmurs against my skin, her voice low and intimate. "You're beautiful, Reema. Inside and out."

I let myself melt into her touch, into the safety of her embrace. As the night stretches on, we lose ourselves in each other, in the quiet intimacy of whispered confessions and tender caresses. And for the first time in years, I feel whole. I feel loved. And I know, deep in my heart, that I've found a home in her arms.

9.
Resilient Canvas

The past three months have been a whirlwind, but for the first time in what feels like forever, life doesn't feel like it's spinning out of control. It feels purposeful. Grounded.

I've been throwing myself into my photography, taking every opportunity, I could to build up the savings I needed for this moment. Weddings, graduation portraits, small events—anything to pay the bills and fund my dream. It was exhausting, but worth it.

In that time, Lila and I made things official. There was no grand announcement or dramatic gesture—just a quiet, mutual understanding that this was it. She's my girlfriend, my partner, my anchor. And with her by my side, I've found a joy I didn't know I was capable of.

Now, as I stand in the doorway of my new apartment, watching my dad haul another box up the stairs, I feel a mix of emotions—excitement, nervousness, pride.

"You're sure this is all of it?" Dad asks, setting the box down with a huff. He straightens, rubbing his lower back dramatically.

"That's the last one, I swear," I say, laughing as I take in the growing mountain of boxes in the corner.

The space is small but perfect. Warm light streams through the big windows, highlighting the freshly painted walls and the hardwood floors that creak just a little underfoot. It's not just an apartment—it's mine.

Dad wipes his hands on his jeans and glances around, a small, satisfied smile tugging at his lips. "You did good, Mimi," he says, his voice soft.

I nod, still trying to take it all in. "I can't believe this is real. It feels like a dream."

"You earned this," he says firmly. "Every bit of it. And if anyone deserves a fresh start, it's you."

I smile at him, my chest tightening with gratitude. It's still a little surreal, having him in my corner like this. For so long, I didn't think I could count on anyone. But now, he's here, hauling boxes and cheering me on.

The sound of a car door closing pulls me out of my thoughts, and I glance out the window to see Lila stepping onto the sidewalk, balancing a bouquet of sunflowers in one hand and a tote bag in the other.

"She's here," I say, my smile widening.

Dad looks out the window and nods approvingly. "She's punctual. I like that."

"Dad," I groan, but I can't help laughing.

By the time Lila reaches the door, I'm already there to greet her. She hands me the flowers with a warm smile before leaning in for a quick kiss. "Welcome home," she says softly.

"Thanks," I whisper, my cheeks flushing.

Lila steps inside, glancing around the apartment. "This place has so much potential," she says, her eyes sparkling. "I can already picture it—your photographs on the walls, plants by the windows, that cozy chair you've been talking about."

"I've been talking about that chair for months," I admit with a laugh.

"You have," she teases, before turning to my dad. "Hi, Mr. Barrett. Thanks for helping Reema move in."

"It's William," he says with a kind smile. "And it's my pleasure. She's earned this."

"I'll never get use to calling you that, but she definitely has." Lila nods, her expression soft.

The three of us spend the rest of the afternoon unpacking, laughing, and planning how to make the apartment feel like home. Dad is surprisingly good at assembling furniture, though he complains the whole time about "missing pieces" that always seem to show up when he's done.

By the time the sun starts to set, the space is beginning to come together. My photographs are propped up against the walls, waiting to be hung. Lila's brought over a few plants and a throw blanket she insists I'll love. Dad has even offered to come back next weekend with a rug he says will "tie the whole place together."

As we sit on the floor, eating takeout and surrounded by half-unpacked boxes, I feel something I haven't felt in years: contentment.

"This is good," Dad says, breaking the comfortable silence. He looks at me, his expression thoughtful. "Seeing you here, happy, with someone who loves you—it's good, Mimi. It's all I've ever wanted for you."

Tears prick my eyes, but I blink them away. "Thanks, Dad. For everything."

He nods, his gaze lingering on me for a moment before shifting to Lila. "And you," he says, his tone warm but serious. "Thank you for loving my daughter the way she deserves to be loved."

Lila smiles, reaching for my hand. "It's easy to love her," she says simply.

That night, after Dad leaves and the apartment is quiet again, Lila and I sit on the couch, looking at the photographs I've set aside for the gallery exhibit.

"You're really doing this," she says, her voice filled with pride.

"I'm terrified," I admit.

She leans in, her lips brushing my cheek. "You're going to be amazing. And your dad and I will be right there, cheering you on."

Her words settle something deep inside me, and for the first time, I feel a flicker of excitement beneath the fear.

Tomorrow, I'll hang my work in the gallery. Tomorrow, I'll share my story with the world.

But tonight, in this small apartment filled with love and hope, I feel like I'm already home.

The next morning comes quickly, the early light creeping through the windows of my apartment. It casts golden streaks across the floor, gently waking me from a peaceful sleep. Lila stirs beside me, her arm draped over my waist, her breath warm against my shoulder. For a moment, I lie still, soaking in the quiet intimacy of the morning—the kind of peace I never thought I'd have.

"You're awake," Lila murmurs, her voice husky with sleep.

I turn to face her, brushing a strand of hair from her face. "Barely. You?"

She smiles lazily, her eyes still half-closed. "I don't think I've ever slept better."

We lie there for a while, neither of us in a hurry to move. It's a stark contrast to the whirlwind of the last few months—quiet, steady, and grounding.

Eventually, reality beckons. The gallery exhibit is tonight, and there's still so much to do. But as I move to get out of bed, Lila pulls me back, her arms wrapping around me.

"Wait," she whispers, her lips brushing against my neck. "Stay a little longer."

I laugh softly, but I let her hold me. "You're a bad influence," I tease, though my heart swells at the warmth of her touch.

"Maybe," she says, her voice low and playful. "But you love it."

And she's right. I do.

By late afternoon, the gallery is bustling with activity. The walls are lined with my photographs, each one carefully selected and arranged to tell a story. My story. Images of light and shadow, pain and resilience, all pieced together to create something whole.

A sign stands proudly in front of my work, bearing the title of my project. For weeks, I'd struggled to decide on a name, unsure of what would capture everything it meant to me. But then, it came to me, clear and certain: "Reema Unveiled."

Dad arrives first, his presence grounding me as always. He walks through the exhibit slowly, his hands clasped behind his back, his expression a mix of pride and emotion.

"You've outdone yourself, Mimi," he says. "These are... incredible."

"Thanks, Dad," I say, my voice barely above a whisper. Hearing those words from him means more than I can say.

Lila arrives a short while later, Asmin by her side. They're both beaming, their excitement infectious. Asmin immediately pulls me into a hug, her enthusiasm bubbling over.

"Reema, this is amazing!" she gushes, stepping back to look at me. "I knew you were talented, but this... This is something else."

Lila doesn't say anything at first. She just stands there, her eyes scanning the room, taking it all in. When she finally turns to me, her eyes are shining.

"You did it," she says softly, her voice filled with awe. "You really did it."

I smile, the knot of anxiety in my chest loosening just a little. "I couldn't have done it without you."

The evening unfolds in a blur of emotions. Strangers and friends alike walk through the gallery, their murmured conversations filling the space. I catch snippets of praise—words like "powerful" and "moving"—but it all feels surreal, like I'm watching it happen to someone else.

At one point, I find myself standing before the centerpiece of the exhibit—a photograph of my hands, scarred but steady, holding a camera. It's simple, but it holds everything I've been through and everything I've become.

"You're incredible, you know that?" Lila's voice pulls me from my thoughts. She stands beside me, her hand slipping into mine. "You've taken everything—everything you've been through—and turned it into something beautiful."

Her words hit me hard, tears pricking at the corners of my eyes. "It doesn't feel real," I admit. "I'm still scared."

"That's okay," she says, squeezing my hand. "Being scared just means you're doing something brave."

I lean into her, letting her strength bolster me. Together, we watch as people pause before the photograph, their expressions contemplative. It's not just my story anymore—it's theirs too.

As the night winds down, Dad finds me again, his face lined with pride and something deeper. "Your mom and I may not always see eye to eye," he says quietly, his voice heavy with emotion. "But I know deep down, she loves you, Mimi. She's proud of you in her own way—even if she doesn't know how to show it."

His words catch me off guard, and for a moment, I'm unsure how to respond. "I just wish..." I start, then trail off, shaking my head.

He places a steady hand on my shoulder. "I know," he says, his voice soft. "But you've shown her, and everyone else, exactly who you are. And no matter what, I'll always be proud of you."

Tears prick at the corners of my eyes, but I manage a smile. "Thanks, Dad," I whisper. His support means more than he'll ever know.

When the last guests leave and the gallery begins to empty, I take a moment to stand in the center of the room, surrounded by my work. Lila and Dad are talking quietly near the door, their voices a comforting backdrop. Asmin is snapping pictures, capturing the moment like I've so often done for others.

For the first time in years, I feel a sense of peace—a quiet, steady certainty that I'm exactly where I'm meant to be.

This is my story. And this is only the beginning.

Don't miss out!

Visit the website below and you can sign up to receive emails whenever Marshatta Rose publishes a new book. There's no charge and no obligation.

https://books2read.com/r/B-A-AJDBD-AZEMF

BOOKS 2 READ

Connecting independent readers to independent writers.